The
Adventures
Of A
Greek Cat
Called Mani

Written by
ANN PEACHEY

ILLUSTRATIONS BY SARAH HUBERT

AuthorHouse™
1663 Liberty Drive
Bloomington, IN 47403
www.authorhouse.com
Phone: 1-800-839-8640

Published by AuthorHouse 09/04/2012

ISBN: 978-1-4685-8206-2 (sc)
978-1-4685-8207-9 (e)

authorHOUSE®

Contents

Illustrations

Introduction

Greece is a very beautiful country. On the mainland there are forests full of bears and wolves, eagles and vultures. There are lakes, rivers, and waterfalls, mountains covered with forests, and fields full of flowers and butterflies. Greece has 6,000 islands, but only 227 have people living on them. But everywhere you go in Greece you will see many cats and dogs, and most of these do not have homes, so they don't have warm beds to sleep in and quite often do not have enough food to eat. This story is set in the villages of Platanos, Pandeli, Aghia Marina and Krithoni on the Island of Leros in the Dodecanese. The names of the tavernas mentioned in Pandeli and Aghia Marina are fictitious.

Once upon a time, an English lady went to live on Leros, and she decided that someone needed to do something to help the many abandoned and unwanted kittens and cats, puppies and dogs. She started a small Animal Welfare Society, Leros Animal Lovers, and devoted her time to running a neutering programme so that there would not be quite so many unwanted kittens and puppies. She soon had a large family _____ and cats who all had stories to tell – if only they could speak. Of the cats mentioned in this st_____ Didi, Mimi and Lucky were part of her cat family living with her at the Leros Cat _____ ged stray living in Platanos. All the other cats and dogs in the story are _____ ation.

_____ ued was named Mani because he was found at Aghia Marina Harbour, a_____ 'LIMANI' pronounced 'LIMAHNEE'. This is Mani's story.

5

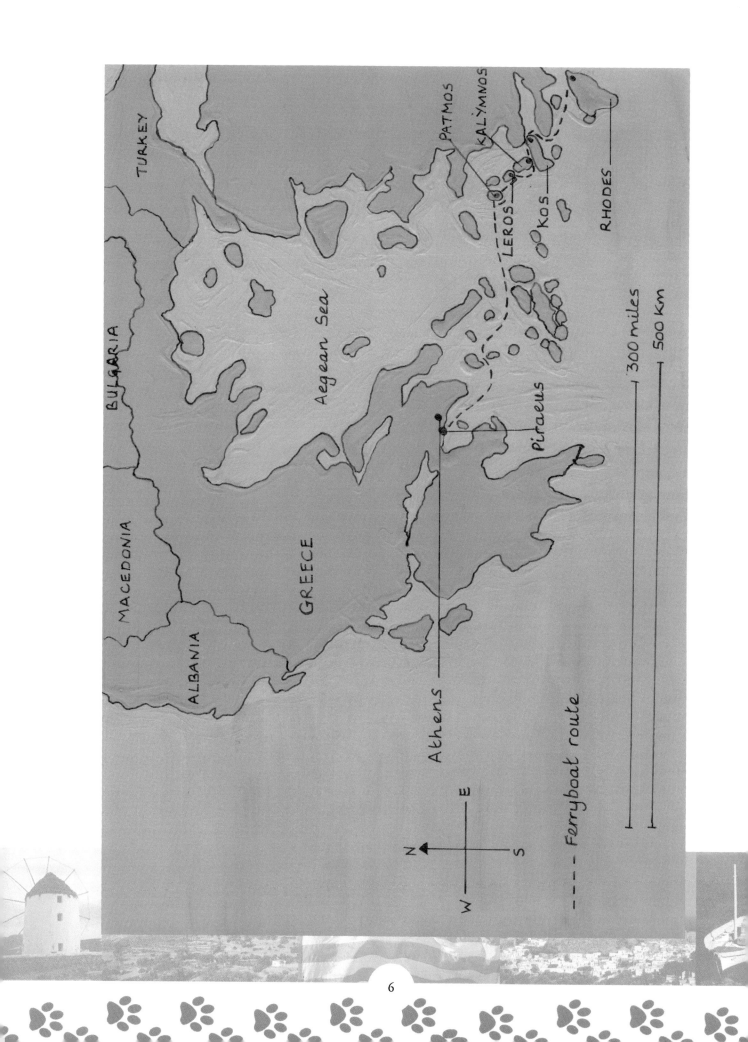

TURKEY

BULGARIA

MACEDONIA

ALBANIA

GREECE

Aegean Sea

PATMOS

KALYMNOS

LEROS

Kos

RHODES

Piraeus

Athens

N

W — E

S

----- Ferryboat route

300 miles

500 Km

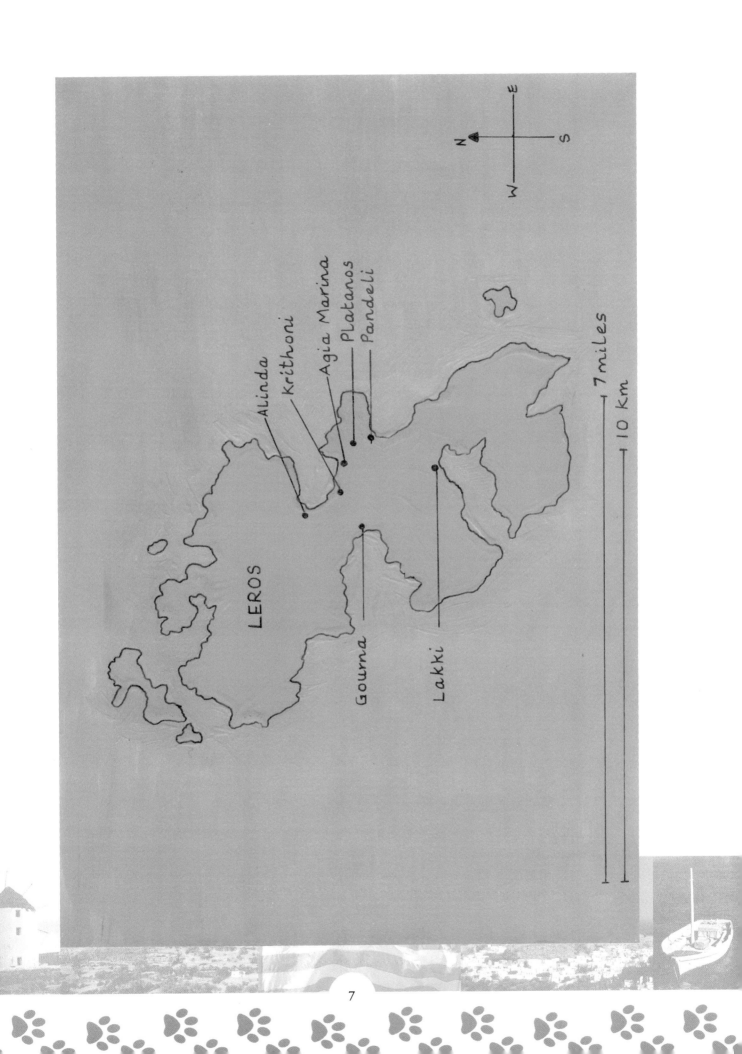

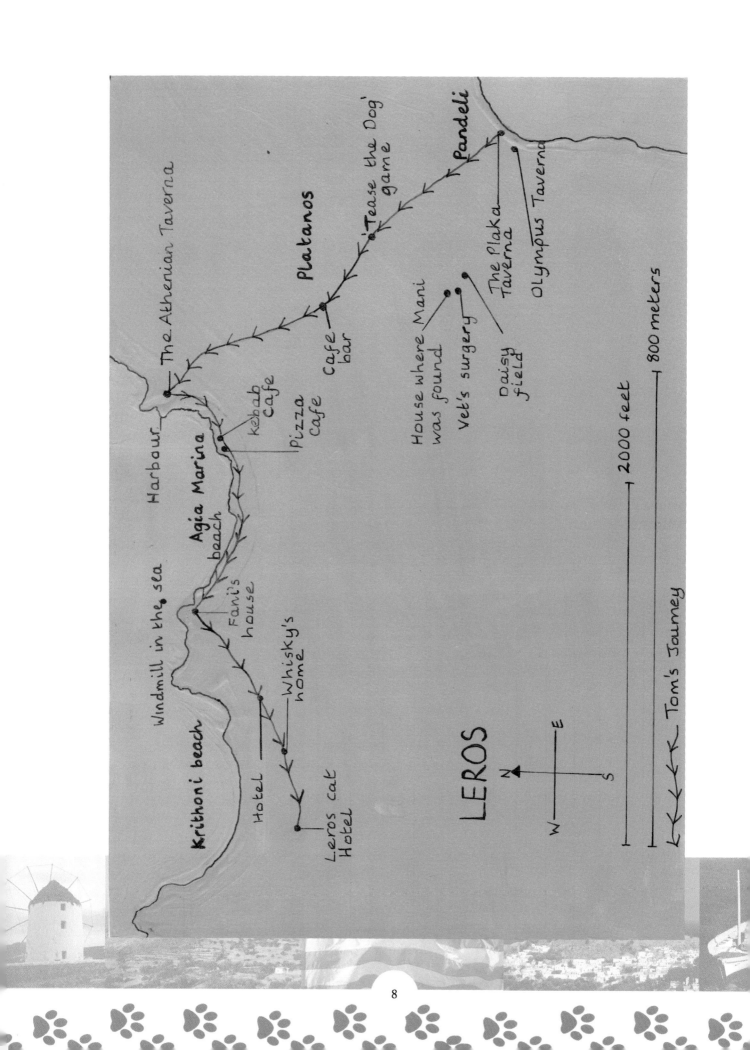

Windmill in the sea

Harbour

The Athenian Taverna

Platanos

'Tease the Dog' game

Pandeli

Agia Marina
beach

Krithoni beach

Fani's
house

Kebab
Cafe

Pizza
Cafe

Cafe
bar

House where Mani
was found

Vet's surgery

Daisy
field

The Plaka
Taverna

Olympus Taverna

Whisky's
home

Hotel

Leros cat
Hotel

LEROS

N
W   E
S

House where Mani
was found

2000 feet

800 meters

Tom's Journey

Chapter 1
Lost And Lonely

Mani cowered under a two-foot high clump of daisies, his little heart pounding with fear. He had not felt this frightened since his mother had been killed. Was that really six months ago? He was the only one of four kittens to survive. The other three had died of starvation before they were four weeks old. His mother had stopped feeding him with her milk and had started giving him solid food, which was not always very easy to find. On the day of the horrific accident, she had taken him to the rubbish bins at the harbour of Aghia Marina on the Island of Leros where they lived, hoping to find some food. She had been leading him back across the road from the rubbish bin where they'd just had dinner, but she was so busy watching Mani to make sure he was following her that she didn't see or hear the lorry that came racing around the bend. Luckily it had missed Mani, and he had dashed across the road and hidden under a pallet of bricks on the harbour, with his little heart pounding fit to burst. And now history was repeating itself. He was lost and alone again.

Last night, for some strange reason, his human Mummy had locked him in the porch with no food, only water. Then this morning she had put him into a new cat box, and placed it on the front seat of her friend's car. On the backseat were four more cat boxes, each with a stray cat inside, and they had all been wailing pitifully. Mani had not been a happy little pussycat! The cat box smelled of new plastic, and although Mummy had put one of his very own blankets in the bottom for him to sit on, it had not smelled of home. He pushed and pushed against the metal bars, but they wouldn't budge. Then the car had stopped, and as the human got out she accidentally knocked the cat box off the seat. Mani gave one final push, the door of the cat box flew open, and he jumped out of the car, dashed across the road and through some gates into a field. He felt the whoosh of a car that just missed his tail, and decided to stay under the daisy bush until his heart beat slowed to normal.

He heard Mummy calling,

"Mani, Mani, it's Mummy. Where are you darling?"

But he was too frightened to come out in case she put him back in that box. Eventually his heart stopped racing and he managed to sleep for a while, though it was nowhere near as comfortable as his bed at home. He woke up in the early afternoon feeling very hungry. He had a good stretch, looked around, and realised with a sense of shock that he was not at home. He was very hungry, as he had not eaten anything since last night, but where was the food? He was used to Mummy coming out of the kitchen every morning with several large plates of food for him and all the other cats that lived with him. He wished his cat mother had taught him how to hunt before she'd been killed. He enjoyed chasing anything that moved, but wasn't sure how to kill things, and the few dead things he'd sampled at home hadn't tasted as good as the cat food that Mummy provided.

Chapter 2
Life On The Wild Side

Mani gingerly ventured out from under the bush and trotted down the field, not knowing which way to go for the best. There was another field below the one he was in, and in the distance he could see the sea. He knew that the sea meant fishermen and fish, so he thought it would be a good idea to try and get down to the lower field and find his way to the sea. He had not gone far when he heard a very loud, menacing, "Grrrrrrr!"

Mani was not used to dogs. The only one he had seen was the little brown puppy that lived in the house opposite to home. He didn't understand their language very well, and it took several seconds for him to realise that this dog was not going to be friendly. He heard the sound of teeth snapping shut, and made a quick decision to run. He ran and ran, with the gnashing of teeth following close behind. He spotted a telegraph pole, swerved and darted up it, as high as his little legs would carry him. He hoped dogs couldn't climb poles. He clung on with his claws dug deep into the wood. When Mani plucked up the courage to look down he realised there were two dogs. Ugly looking things with big, heavy faces and small, evil eyes, and tiny ears that stuck up in the air, which made them look even more frightening. Their bodies were large and out of proportion to their short legs. One was black and white, and the other brown with dark marks. They were snarling, growling and salivating, teeth bared, and they were jumping at least four feet in the air in an attempt to reach him.

Mani hung on as though his life depended on it, knowing that if he slipped he would fall right into the jaws of one of those slathering beasts. He lost track of time, but the muscles in his legs were aching and burning, and felt as though they were being torn apart. His claws were slowly losing their grip. He slipped a couple of inches, and tried to dig his claws further into the wood. It splintered, and he slipped another few inches. Then, he heard "Yowl, yowl" coming from the top of the field, and there in the distance stood a large, very battle scarred old black cat. The dogs turned in unison, and took off after the old tomcat.

Slowly, slowly, Mani inched his way to the bottom of his pole and almost collapsed with exhaustion. He could hear the dogs barking in the distance, and hoped that his saviour managed to outrun them. He headed back to his daisy bush. He didn't feel very hungry now and just wanted to rest. He was exhausted and fell asleep, all thought of food forgotten. He slept and slept, dreaming of home. The horrors went away in his sleep, so he didn't want to wake up too soon. Finally, he stirred, stretched, and once again had that awful sinking feeling when he remembered where he was. He had slept through the night, and the sun was just rising over the imposing castle that stood on top of the hill overlooking the village and harbour of Aghia Marina and the small fishing village of Pandeli, with the town of Platanos in the middle. At home he would have thought how beautiful it looked, but he had more important things on his mind – food.

Chapter 3
Mani Meets His Saviour

Mani was just wondering if he dared try and go down to the sea again in the hope that he might find a fish or two, when he heard, "Mrow, Mrow," and there was the old black cat. At close quarters he looked even worse for wear. His ears were torn, and his face covered with bloody scratches. He had a wound on his neck that had not quite healed, and he stank. Mani didn't know whether to be pleased to see a familiar face, or to be frightened of it!

"Lesson number one, kid—you shouldn't mess with Pit Bulls you know! They kill little cats like you, and dogs too! I haven't seen you around here before. Have you been abandoned? You look too pretty and well fed to be a stray. In fact, you look like a special breed of cat, Turkish Van I think it is, with your long white fur, and ginger cap and tail."

"I don't think I am," said Mani, "but it's nice of you to say so, and thank you so much for saving my life. I don't know how I shall ever be able to repay you. I'm lost. I jumped out of a car yesterday morning and all I want to do is go home, but I don't know where it is."

"What were you doing in a car?"

"I'm not too sure, but I did hear Mummy say something about it being time to neuter me, and as I jumped out of the car I recognised the smell of the animal doctor's surgery. If Mummy had been with me in the car I don't think I would have bothered to escape, but I thought she didn't want me any more, and had given me away to her friend."

"Do you have any idea where 'home' is?" asked Tom.

"Not really. It's very beautiful—a big house with a garden and fields all around it with lots of trees to climb, and mice and insects to chase. We can see the *Kastro* (Castle) in the distance, and from the top of the shed we can see the sea. Twenty-eight cats live there. We have our own room, and a cat house outside with three separate apartments, plus lots of beds and boxes to sleep in. There is always food. Sometimes Mummy's very busy looking after stray cats. She has a lot of cages and keeps the strays in them for a few days. The strays always smell funny when they arrive, like the doctor's surgery. There are some other cats who just come to the house to eat. Some of them look a bit like you. Oh, I'm sorry, I didn't mean to be rude, but you do look as though you've been in a few fights!"

"Mm! Life is tough in the wild. I have a couple of friends down in Pandeli who disappeared for a day or two and came back with the top of their left ears clipped off, but they are still very handsome fellows. They don't get involved in many fights now and they've given up the ladies for some reason, and I've noticed they no longer smell like tomcats. You're a bit too young to know much about that yet. Your 'home' sounds fantastic. Were you born there?"

"No," said Mani. "Some tourists chased me out from under a pallet of bricks at Aghia Marina Harbour when I was about four weeks old. My mother had just been run over by a car, and I was so frightened. They gave me to a lady. I remember being carried inside her T-shirt, which had a map of Leros on it, and Leros Animal Lovers written across it. I cried and cried, and she spoke to me so nicely. It was very warm and cosy in there too. We walked quite a long way, and after a while I couldn't smell the sea so strongly. There were different smells—trees, flowers, and lots of things I'd never seen or smelt before. Then I was told we were 'home'. And I've lived there ever since—until today, and now I'm lost again."

"Shush! What's that?" said Tom.

"Mani, Mani, darling, where are you? Please come out, I want to take you home. Oh, I'm so worried about you. Mani! Mani!"

"That's Mummy," said Mani. "But I don't know what to do. If I go to her she might put me back in that box and give me away."

"Why would she do that?"

"Well, she does have a lot of cats, so maybe she's decided to give some of us away. I don't know. I don't know what to do. I want to go home."

"Stick with me, kid. I'll see you're all right. Life's not too bad on the wild side. I can show you where to find food, and there's always somewhere warm and dry to sleep. There are a few houses around here with cats, so we can steal some food sometimes. I'll show you the ropes," assured Tom.

So, Mani stayed hidden under the daisy bush and his poor, worried Mummy went home again, and shed a few more tears. Later that day she had a brain wave. She made up a poster with Mani's photo on it. It wasn't a very up to date photo as it was taken when he was about five months old, and now he was seven months, but it showed up his colouring well, and his face hadn't changed much as he had grown. The poster said that she would offer a reward of 50,000 drachmas (approximately £100) to anyone who found him. She hurried to the Photography Shop and asked them to make lots of photocopies of the poster in colour. She put the posters up outside the Town Hall, the Post Office and several shops, and on telegraph poles and trees in Platanos, Pandeli and Aghia Marina. Mani was quite a famous little cat! But still lost.

Chapter 4
The Dangers Of Life On The Wild Side

Tom took Mani under his paw, and led him through the fields and down to Pandeli. They were heading for the fish market, as Tom had explained to him that there were often some tiny fishes scattered about just asking to be eaten. Suddenly, Mani stopped. He caught the whiff of meat. Where was it coming from? Then he spotted a large, juicy meatball sitting on the ground near a chicken run. He was just about to take a mouthful, when he remembered Tom, and decided it was most impolite to start eating without his new friend.

"Tom, look what I've found!"

Mani's teeth were closing on the meatball, when Tom shouted,

"No! Leave it!"

The urgency in his voice penetrated Mani's hunger, and he stopped.

"Why? It smells so good and we're so hungry!"

Tom sat down by the meatball, and rested his paw on it. He looked long and hard at Mani, and said,

"Mani. Lesson number two. Never, ever eat anything without checking it very carefully first. There are some very unpleasant humans around here who poison cats and dogs. Their favourite way is to stuff poison—usually something called organophosphate—into a chunk of smelly, tasty food, like a fish or a meatball. I've lost a few good friends over the years, and it is not a nice way to go I can tell you. They died writhing in agony. I can still hear their screams in my head. So listen good, kid, and watch and learn. First, you gently tear it apart, being careful not to put your claws inside it. If some black powder falls out of it, DO NOT EAT IT!! And look . . . . . black powder! If the fish or meat is solid in the middle, and doesn't smell odd in any way, it's OK to eat. But if in doubt, leave it out!"

"That's the second time you've saved my life!" said Mani in a frightened little voice.

"Ah, well. That's what us old'uns are here for. To try to teach you youngsters a thing or two! Now, come on, follow me, and next time you see something interesting, think first before you touch it."

Tom decided to stop at the Olympus Taverna on the beach, before visiting the fish market. It was a beautifully warm, sunny day, and although it was still only early April, there were a few tables out on the beach, and a dozen or so people having lunch.

"Now, kid," said Tom, "as you can see, I'm no oil painting, while you certainly are! What we do is this. You go around the tables, mewing pitifully. Rub around their legs— though not the ones with dark trousers on—they don't like that much! Gaze up at them with a sorrowful expression in your eyes. Then meow again. Works every time. Don't snatch the food, and don't, whatever you do, scratch them! They don't like that either. I'll stay out of sight behind this tree. Don't forget to save something tasty for me."

"It won't be poisoned, will it?" asked Mani.

"No way, kid. The humans are eating it, aren't they?"

Mani worked well. There were cries of, "What a gorgeous little cat!"

"He looks well fed!"

"He does seem a bit hungry though."

"Oh, how cute he is!"

He saved some tit-bits for Tom, so they both ate well. The food at The Olympus was always good, as Tom knew very well. Unfortunately though, his days of begging for food were over. Everywhere he went now he was chased away.

"What a horrible looking cat," people would say, "and he smells too!"

Very rarely, a human would see something special in him, maybe a hint of what he used to be when he was younger, and he would be given some food and, if he was lucky and the human was a cat lover, a caress or two.

Chapter 5
Out Of The Frying Pan Into The Fire!

Mani and Tom curled up on the beach in the shade of a jacaranda tree and slept off their lunch. Later in the day they walked up the hill to the field with the daisy bushes and Tom showed Mani where he usually slept at night. There were some old wooden sheds at the end of the field, and although they were now in ruins, they provided shelter from the wind and rain. And so the next two days went by, with Tom taking care of Mani. They dined at the fish market every morning, and one evening they tried their luck at The Plaka Taverna. Mani could tempt food out of anyone!

That evening at The Plaka was a special one, and there were many tourists eating there. All the tables were full, both inside the taverna and on the beach. It was the night of the full moon, and everyone knew that Pandeli was the best place to be to watch the moon rise. Tom and Mani sat on the beach looking towards the cliffs at the end of Pandeli. Suddenly, a glimmer of golden red appeared at the edge of the cliff. It grew and grew until it looked like a very large red disc suspended above the sea. Mani couldn't believe his eyes. He had never seen anything quite so beautiful and he thought he might even be able to touch it if he reached out with his paw. As the moon continued to move slowly, slowly across the sky, its colour gradually changed from red to silver, and where the glow from the moon was reflected onto the sea, it looked just like a silver road stretching from the beach to the little island of Aghios Kyriakos. Tom said he tried to walk on it once, intending to visit the island, but instead he got his feet very wet. The night wore on, and the two cats sat on the sand bathed in moon glow until it was time to go home to bed.

On the fourth night, Tom decided he felt too tired to go all the way down to Pandeli for food, and suggested going across the road to a house which just happened to be next door to the animal doctor's surgery, where Mani had escaped from the car. A dog and several cats lived at this house, so there was usually some food just waiting to be eaten. Mani was very frightened of crossing this road after his narrow escape, but Tom told him to stick closely beside him, and run like mad when he shouted, "Go!" They made it to the courtyard, and sure enough, by the front door there was a dish of dried food and a bowl of fresh water. Mani had just taken his first mouthful, when he heard the door open, and a boy of about 9 years old came out of the house.

"*Mops, ella doh! Ella doh, Mani! (*Pussycat, come here! Come here, Mani)," he called.

Mani recognised the words, but he couldn't think how this boy, whom he had never seen in his life, knew his name. Instead of running off, he was curious, and allowed the boy to stroke him. He had got used to strangers touching him when he was begging for food down in Pandeli. But suddenly, the boy grabbed him round the middle and dashed into the house with him.

"Meow, meow, Tom, help!"

But Tom was long gone, straight across the road, and into the field. No way was he going to risk being caught by a human! The boy put Mani into a small bedroom and closed the door. Mani tried everything he could to get out, but he was trapped. The boy brought him some food, water, and a litter tray in case he needed to go to the toilet. Mani was used to litter trays at home, as there were two in the Cats' Room.

Chapter 6
Mani Hears A Familiar Voice

The boy wanted to make friends with Mani and said softly, "*Mani, parakalo, ella doh. Eisai poli omorfi gataki Mani.* (Mani, please come here. You are a very beautiful little cat, Mani.)"

But Mani decided it was safer to stay hidden under the bed until the boy had gone. What he was going to do now he just did not know. Once it had gone quiet and he was alone he crept out from under the bed and ate some of the food, and then he did what all cats do best – he curled up on the bed and went to sleep! He dreamed of home, of playing in the fields, and climbing the almond trees, and especially he dreamed of his Mummy. In his dream she was cuddling him and saying how gorgeous he was. He awoke suddenly. It was morning already. And then he heard voices. It sounded a little like his Mummy's voice, though she was speaking in Greek.

"I must still be dreaming," he thought.

Then the door opened. Mani shot back under the bed and cried with fear.

"Mani, come on out darling, Mummy has come to take you home."

He was still very unsure of what he should do. Could he trust her? Where was Tom? He had always seemed to know the answers, but now Mani was alone and had to make his own decisions.

"It might be better if you go out, and leave me alone with him," he heard his Mummy say to the boy. The door closed, the bed was moved, and a dish of sardines placed on the floor. Mani just couldn't resist poking his little head out from under the bed to have a look. And, there was his Mummy, smiling down at him. She quickly grabbed him by the scruff of the neck before he could dart back under the bed, and gave him the biggest cuddle and kiss. But then, horror of horrors, she put him in a cat cage. This was even worse than the plastic cat box! What now? He was convinced that she was going to give him away! She thanked the boy very much, handed over the reward, said goodbye and carried the cage to her motorbike. She carefully fastened it to the carrier on the back of the bike, and set off down the road.

Poor Mani, after all he'd been through, now he was bouncing around in a cage on the back of a motorbike! But, at least it was his Mummy's bike, so maybe they were going home. Then he smelled that special aroma—a mixture of sea, flowers, and trees. Home! Mummy carried him into the house in the cage, and then gently lifted him out, and gave him another big cuddle. She was crying with relief, and Mani, being a cat, decided that if he played his cards right, he might do very well out of this. A rub around the legs, a pathetic meow or two, and he knew he'd be spoiled rotten and given the very best food—canned, not the dried stuff—and maybe even some expensive fish! He was very, very happy to be home again, but he did wish he could do something for Tom, because he knew that without his help he probably wouldn't have lived to tell the tale.

Chapter 7
Home Sweet Home

Next day, Mani was lazing in the sun with Didi and Mimi, the ginger and white twins, Lucky, who was white with long, silky fur, and Sylvester who had short white fur with a black tail and black patches on his face. Mani told them all about his big adventure and how lucky he was that Tom had been there to save his life—twice.

"I wish I could do something in return to help him. If only I could get a message to him and ask him to come and visit me here. I am sure if he saw where we live and how lucky we are to have Mummy to look after us and give us such good food and a choice of warm, comfortable beds to sleep in, he would want to stay here and never go back to living wild in Pandeli," said Mani.

Sylvester looked thoughtful for a moment, and then said, "What about the GCG? The Great Cat Grapevine?"

"What is that?" asked Mani.

"Well, I often go to visit some friends on the other side of our valley. A couple of them regularly visit the harbour at Aghia Marina when the fishing boats come in. They have friends in Aghia Marina who sometimes go up to Platanos, and there are cats in Platanos who visit Pandeli. You see—the Great Cat Grapevine. News travels from one cat to another and from one place to another. Once Tom gets your message, he can easily find his way here with the help of the GCG."

"Oh, what a wonderful idea!" shouted Mani. "Please talk to your friends across the valley as soon as you can, and then all we can do is wait and see if Tom finds me."

That night Sylvester went out on the prowl as usual, hunting for a mouse or two, and then he visited one of his friends, Whisky, a pretty black and white cat, and told him all about Mani and Tom. Next day at the harbour in Aghia Marina, Whisky passed the message on to Big Red, a handsome dark ginger tabby cat, who said he would be going up to Platanos sometime soon.

A couple of days later Big Red was strolling along the road to Platanos and suddenly remembered he had a message to pass on. He met Long John Silver outside the Café Bar.

Long John had dirty white fur with a grey tail and eye patch, and he only had three legs. He had been involved in an accident with a car and had almost died from his wounds, but Mani's human Mummy had managed to catch him and had taken him to the animal doctor who had said that unfortunately he couldn't save his front left leg. But Long John soon recovered from the operation and discovered he could run and jump, catch mice, and fight other cats just as easily with three legs as with four. He said he would run down to Pandeli later that evening and try to find this Tom and pass on Mani's message.

Later that day, true to his word, Long John ran down to Pandeli and headed for the fish market. There was no sign of a cat answering Tom's description, so he strolled along the beach towards The Olympus Taverna, and on the beach outside the taverna sat a cat that looked as though he could be Tom.

"Excuse me, Sir," he said as politely as he could. "Is your name Tom, and do you know a kitten called Mani?"

Tom turned round and saw a dirty white cat with only three legs. He had also lost the tip of his left ear.

"Who's asking?" he said, "and how do you know Mani?"

Long John explained that Mani was trying to get a message to him by the GCG.

"Nothing wrong with him, I hope? He's a nice little kid, and he was very homesick. I thought his human had found him and taken him home," said Tom.

"Yes, he is home again, but he wants to know if you would like to go and visit him and meet the rest of his family. He thought you might like to have a little holiday in Krithoni, and have a change of scene from Pandeli," said Long John.

"Well, I am not too sure about that. It is quite a long way for an old cat like me, and I have never been much further than here in Pandeli and up the hill to Platanos a few times. I think I'm a bit too old for travelling, and I'm not sure I can find Krithoni."

"Oh, that will be easy. You just use the GCG like we did. I'll take you up to Platanos, and from there Big Red will go with you down to Aghia Marina and introduce you to Whisky, who will take you to his side of the Krithoni valley. I expect you can spend the night there if you want. And then Whisky will run across the valley to Mani's house and fetch Sylvester, who will escort you to Mani and his family. From what everyone has said, Mani's human will make you welcome. She takes in lots of waifs and strays. Oh, not that you are one of those, Sir!" said Long John.

Tom looked thoughtful, and then said, "Maybe a holiday would do me good. They say a change is as good as a rest, and I would like to check up on Mani. If you can manage all this travelling from Platanos to Pandeli and back with just three legs, I think I might be able to make it on four, even if they are getting a bit old and stiff. How about we leave from here tomorrow morning about ten o'clock? That will give me time to find some breakfast, and I can have a good night's sleep tonight so I'll have lots of energy tomorrow for the journey."

"Oh, that's great. Mani will be pleased," said Long John. "I'll be here tomorrow morning at ten. I'll get a message to Big Red and make sure he'll be waiting for us in Platanos. Have a good night."

Long John made his way up to Platanos, asking all the cats he met to pass on a message to Big Red in Aghia Marina telling him that he and Tom would arrive in Platanos the next day at about noon.

Chapter 8
Tom's Holiday

The following morning Tom woke up at about eight o'clock. The sun was shining as usual. He stretched and yawned, and then remembered that this was the day he was going on holiday for the first time in his long life. He wandered up the road to the fish market and luckily found three little fishes on the ground. His next stop was at a house not far from the fish market where he knew he would find some milk and dried food, if the other cats hadn't got there first. He was lucky, and after his milk and biscuits he had time for a short nap before meeting Long John.

"Wake up, Tom. It's me, Long John. Time to set off for Platanos."

Tom yawned and stretched. "I must have nodded off after my breakfast," he said, "but I'm ready to go. I'm looking forward to going on holiday!"

The two cats set off up the road to Platanos, chatting about all sorts of cat things: where to find the best fish, the easiest way to catch a mouse, how to avoid being chased by dogs.

"Talking of dogs," said Long John, "have you ever played 'Tease the Dog'?"

"No. What on earth is that? I've had a few fights with dogs over the years and luckily managed to win, but I've never heard of that game," replied Tom.

"I'll show you. If we jump over that wall and head up the hill through some fields, we'll come to a house with a huge garden, and in one corner there is a tree, and chained to the tree is a large dog. He has a very bad temper and is the perfect bait for playing 'Tease the Dog'."

A few minutes later, Long John whispered, "Here we are. Keep as quiet as you can. We'll jump onto the top of wall over there, and then we can see the dog and check that he is chained up. Very important to check that first, as we don't want him to chase us!"

When they reached the top of the garden wall, Tom looked down and saw an enormous black and brown dog. He thought it might be a Rottweiler, or at the very least, related to a Rottweiler, and he looked mean. Tom did feel a little sorry for the animal though, as he was chained to a tree, and the chain was only about 1 meter long. The poor dog had worn the grass down to the earth around the bottom of the tree by going round and round in circles. He thought that Mani's human Mummy would be very unhappy to see a dog living like this.

Long John said, "OK, he is definitely chained up today, so here we go. Watch me. The plan is that we sit here and sunbathe for a few minutes. He'll see us soon and start to get a bit upset. Then we'll jump down and run towards him, making sure we stop before he can reach us."

After a couple of minutes Long John jumped down and ran towards the dog, and the poor animal leapt towards the cat, barking insanely, but, of course, he was brought to a sudden stop by his short chain. Tom decided to stay where he was. Although he didn't like dogs, especially after one had managed to grab his tail a few years ago when he was trying to run away from it, Tom did think it was rather cruel to tease the poor creature. Long John soon got bored with the game and ran back up the wall to Tom.

"You didn't join in the fun!" said Long John.

"Well, I know I am older than you, and maybe just a little wiser, but it seemed to me that it's rather cruel to tease the poor dog like that. He must have a horrible life, spending most of it chained to a tree. Dogs are fair game when they are loose, and I've ripped a nose or two over the years when a dog hasn't moved quite quickly enough to avoid my claws, but that was different because they were running free and chasing me, and I was protecting myself. Maybe we can think up some new games. Fishing can be fun. I have a friend in Pandeli who sometimes manages to hook a fish out of the sea with his sharp claws."

"That sounds like a good game and it could be fun, especially if we are lucky enough to catch something to eat," said Long John. "Aghia Marina would be a good place to try our paws at fishing. We had better get going again, as Big Red will be waiting for us."

They hurried up the steps to Platanos and headed for the Café Bar. Sat in a corner under a bush was a large ginger cat, and he too had lost the tip of his left ear.

"Ah, there's Big Red, on time as usual," said Long John.

"Hey, Long John, that's another two cats I've met with a bit of their left ears missing – you, and now Big Red. I have a few friends in Pandeli who have lost a bit of their left ears," remarked Tom.

"Funny you should notice that. When I came back from the animal doctor after losing my leg, I noticed that I had lost the tip of my left ear, and for some reason I no longer wanted to chase the ladies. Big Red disappeared for a couple of days some time ago and came back minus a bit of his ear, and he'd lost interest in the girls. And I know some beautiful lady cats who came back from the animal doctor with clipped left ears, and they have no interest in the men now, and haven't given birth to any kittens since. I must say they all look so much more beautiful now, plump and healthy, because they don't have to spend their lives trying to bring up four or five kittens at least three times a year. And the male cats look much stronger and healthier afterwards too."

Big Red stood up, had a good, long stretch, and then strolled towards them through the tables outside the Café Bar.

"Hi there Long John. This must be the famous Tom you told me about. Pleased to meet you, Tom. That was a good thing you did helping out young Mani. So, you are off on holiday to Krithoni I hear. Next stop is Aghia Marina. It will be lunchtime soon, and I thought we could visit the harbour and see if there are any fish. There are several good tavernas there too, with lots of tourists, and we just might be able to beg for a few tasty morsels. We had better get going now, or we'll miss lunch. See you soon, Long John."

"Thank you very much for helping me out, Big Red," said Tom. "Everyone is being so kind and helpful to an old cat. I haven't been anywhere other than Pandeli and up here to Platanos a few times, so it is quite an adventure for an oldie like me. And thank you too, Long John. Hopefully, I'll see you again soon and we can try out that fishing game."

Big Red and Tom went around to the back of the Café Bar and started to make their way down to Aghia Marina, but not on the road as there were too many motorbikes, cars and lorries, and it could be very dangerous. They made their way through gardens and courtyards, jumping over walls, stopping to say "Hello" to a few cats on the way, and keeping well clear of any dogs they saw. Though most of these were chained to kennels, oil barrels or trees in their humans' gardens, and looked very unhappy.

Tom smelled the sea again, and soon they arrived at the harbour of Aghia Marina. It was bigger than the fishing village of Pandeli with many more boats moored. There was also a large ferryboat docked at the end of the harbour. Tom had not seen one of those before and he could not believe that anything so enormous could float on the sea. Then he had an even bigger surprise, when he saw some cars going into its mouth.

"Goodness me! A boat that eats cars!" he shouted.

Big Red replied, "No, it's a ferryboat and I have heard that it goes from here to Athens and back, and it carries many cars, lorries and humans. It also brings a lot of interesting stuff here, like cat food for instance. So, don't go exploring on board or you could wake up in Athens! Let's stop at The Athenian Taverna and try our luck with the tourists. The owner quite likes cats, so we won't get chased off, unless one of the tourists doesn't like the look of us."

"Mrrow, mrrow, prrrr, prrrr," said Big Red and Tom in unison, as they strolled towards one of the tables.

"Oh, look. What a beautiful big ginger cat. Here Ginger, have a piece of meat. Oh, the old black one is in a bit of a state, poor old thing. Here Blacky, you can have two pieces," said Tourist number one.

Tourist number two picked up a couple of fish heads from his plate, and called, "Come here cats, one each, as long as you don't scratch me!"

Later, Big Red and Tom sat by the sea licking themselves all over and savouring the last of the fish and meat taste.

"That was a good lunch," said Tom. "I must come here again. Thank you Big Red. I like the look of Aghia Marina and there seem to be some cat friendly humans around too."

"Don't relax too much. There are a few humans here that will throw something at us or kick us if they get the chance. We have been lucky today," said Big Red. "We'll have a nap on the beach and then we'll go and find Whisky. He's usually along the road near the supermarket, which just happens to be across the road from a café that specialises in kebabs. And next door to that is one that makes pizzas. We might be able to find a teatime snack. I'm sure we'll be feeling a bit peckish again after our nap."

A couple of hours later, Big Red woke up and stretched, and then tapped Tom with his paw to wake him up. Tom stirred, and then he had a good stretch too.

"I am feeling a bit tired and achy now," said Tom. "Let's go and find your friend Whisky. I hope it isn't too much further to Krithoni as I am looking forward to having a very long sleep when I get there. I want to be at my best tomorrow when I meet Mani again."

"It's not too far if you go across the fields and gardens and not on the road. Whisky knows all the short cuts. Let's get going again."

They trotted around the harbour, past the big ferryboat, which was just getting ready to leave for Athens. They ran along the harbour wall by the sea to the supermarket, and outside the Kebab Café sat Whisky, a pretty black and white cat with a bit missing from his left ear, who was munching away on a succulent piece of pork.

"Hello there, Big Red. You made it. And this must be Tom. Hi there. Sit down and tuck in if you're hungry. I managed to grab a whole kebab without being seen, so there is plenty for the three of us. And then we must get started for Krithoni. My human will be wondering where I am. She gets a bit worried if I disappear for too long," said Whisky.

Nobody spoke for several minutes, as they were much too busy enjoying the tastiest kebab that Tom had ever eaten. After cleaning their whiskers, Whisky said, "Right, time to go. Thanks Big Red, and watch the traffic going back to Platanos."

Whisky and Tom ran along the lane by the Aghia Marina Beach passing the Windmill that sat in the sea at the end of the bay. They stopped to say hello to several cats lounging in a fishing boat outside an old house. Whisky explained to Tom that the house belonged to his human's son, Fani, who, like his mother, Maria, had adopted several stray cats. They stopped at the top of the lane to make sure that it was safe to cross the road, and then they headed inland away from the sea, following a path that went uphill past several small houses with large gardens.

"We don't go near the road any more now," said Whisky. "The countryside is really pretty around here. There are groves of olive trees, flowers, and lots of mice and rabbits too. It is very good for hunting all the way from here to Krithoni. I sometimes take a tasty little mouse or rabbit home to my human as a present to say thank you for caring for me, but for some reason she never seems too pleased! Humans are a bit strange aren't they? But I know I'm lucky to have one. Mani has fallen on his paws too. His human is quite amazing and looks after so many cats. Her house is like a Cat Hotel. You must have had a hard time of it, living on the wild side all your life. A holiday at Mani's will do you the world of good."

"I've spent most of my life trying to avoid humans, except when I try my luck at the tavernas," said Tom. "I had several bad experiences when I was younger. Met the wrong humans obviously. For a long time I thought they were all the same and not to be trusted. But meeting Mani has made me think again. Maybe there are a few that we can trust."

Eventually, they reached the top of the hill and Whisky said, "See that old house down there? That's where I live. My human feeds a few of us, and she has a big dog too, but he is very friendly, and just a big softy at heart. He was abandoned on Krithoni beach when he was a puppy. His parents were hunting dogs, but their human didn't want any more dogs, so they left the puppy on the beach one night. Luckily, my human found him. She also keeps chickens so there are always plenty of fresh eggs to eat. Do you see that little lane beyond my house? Mani lives in that big cottage with steps leading up to it from the lane, the very long house with the orchard in front of it, and the fields at the side and behind it. If your eye sight is good you might just see some of his family sitting on the veranda and making the most of the last of the sun before it sets."

"Wow! That is quite a place," said Tom. "I am so glad I decided to have a holiday. I am really looking forward to tomorrow. I do hope Mani's human will make me welcome and won't be put off by my scruffy looks."

Chapter 9
Tom Meets Mani's Mummy And Makes A Big Decision

Tom woke up at dawn, just as the sun was rising. He stretched and then blinked.

"Where am I?" he said. "Oh, yes, I'm on holiday and today I am going to meet Mani again and his human. But right now I am hungry and thirsty."

Right on cue he heard a female voice calling, "*Ella mops!* (Here pussies!)," and he heard the rattle of dried food being poured into a metal dish. Tom peered around the corner, and there was Whisky and five other cats of assorted colours and sizes all crowded around a large metal bowl. One of these cats was white with some black patches on his face and a black tail. His front left leg was bent at an odd angle.

"Oh, there you are," said Whisky. "Come and have some breakfast. There is enough for us all this morning. Sometimes my human doesn't have enough money to buy us food, so she cooks pasta and mixes it with leftovers. But this morning we have some biscuits, which are quite tasty. Let me introduce you to Sylvester. He'll take you across the valley to Mani. His human doesn't get up quite as early as mine, so it will be a little while before he wakes up and has breakfast. If you time it right you might be lucky today and have two breakfasts. That's why Sylvester sometimes comes here first."

The cat with the bent left leg said, "Hi Tom, we meet at last. I'm Sylvester. Mani hasn't stopped talking about you and your adventures in Pandeli. He'll be so happy to see you again."

"Glad to meet you Sylvester," said Tom. "What happened to your leg?"

"Oh, I had an accident when I was a kitten. I ran out into the road and this thing on wheels hit me. Luckily, I can run, jump, climb and fight with it. Just looks a bit odd that's all, and it aches sometimes when it rains."

Tom tucked into the biscuits, which were very tasty and a pleasant change from fish and scraps from the fish market and tavernas in Pandeli. Soon it was time to set off for Mani's house. Tom said goodbye to Whisky and promised to visit him soon.

Sylvester led the way across the valley, stopping for a moment to gaze across to Mani's home. A few minutes later they arrived at the gate leading to the orchard in front of the house. They ran up the steps to the veranda, but there were no cats there. Sylvester led Tom to the end of the veranda, and there under a table, were three cats fast asleep in a box. Under a window was a large kennel that was divided into three separate compartments. This was Villa Felix, a three-roomed apartment house made especially for cats. Each apartment contained a sleeping cat.

"Whisky was right when he told you we don't get up very early around here," said Sylvester. "That door goes into the Cats' Room and we can go in and out through the little door which Mummy calls a cat flap. Yes, we have our very own room with a large bed and lots of cat beds and boxes to sleep in, plus food and water available all day and all night. There is a wardrobe and a table, and some of the cats prefer to sleep up high and climb to the top of the wardrobe. We also have lots of toys to play with, and a climbing frame with a special place to sharpen our claws, though most of us prefer to use the door frame. The toys are great fun in the winter when it's raining and we don't want to go out. I'll put my head through the cat flap and see if Mani is in there. Hey, Mani, are you awake yet? I have a surprise for you."

"Prrr, mrrow. Who is that at the door?" said Mani in a sleepy voice. "It's a bit early for visitors."

Then he heard a familiar voice say, "Hey kid, it's me, Tom. I decided to take you up on your offer of a holiday. You are a lazy lot of cats at the Leros Cat Hotel. We've been up for hours."

Mani jumped up and rushed to the door. He was so excited he completely forgot to have his morning stretch.

"Hello Tom. It is so good to see you again. How are you? You are looking very well. You are just in time for breakfast. I can hear Mummy coming now. She always comes into our room first with food and fresh water, and then cleans out our litter trays. Next she goes out to the barn and fetches more food for the cats that like to sleep outside. It takes her quite a while every day. She never has her breakfast until she has fed us. We usually have some canned food mixed with pasta as well as biscuits."

The door opened and in walked Mani's human Mummy, still in her dressing gown, struggling to carry four large dishes of food. She put them down, picked up the water bowls and disappeared to the bathroom for fresh water, then she unlocked the door to the veranda and carried out the litter trays. She did a quick head count to check that all the cats were present and correct.

"And who are you?" she said, when she spotted Tom. "I haven't seen you before. You are a bit of a tatty old cat aren't you, with your torn ears and battle scars. But you have a nice face. Come here and let me stroke you, or are you too nervous?"

Tom looked up at her, and although he wasn't too sure about letting her touch him (she was a human after all), he thought she had a kind face, and it was obvious that all the other cats trusted her.

"Mrrow, mrrow, mrrow. Prr, Prr. I think I'll try rubbing round your legs a bit first, if you don't mind, then maybe I'll let you touch me," he said. "Oh yes, you do have a nice touch. You've found that place behind my ear where I love to be scratched."

"You are a friendly old puss aren't you?" said Mani's Mummy. "As you are an old tomcat maybe I'll call you Tommy. If you promise not to fight with the other cats you can stay if you want. There is plenty of room for one more. And you do seem to be very friendly with Mani."

Tom, Mani and the other cats decided there had been enough chatting. It was time to eat. Once breakfast was over, they all sat in their favourite places on the veranda and on the garden walls and proceeded to have a good wash. Each paw was given a good licking, then they washed behind their ears, next it was the turn of their tummies and sides, and finally under their tails. When bath time was over they wandered out to the veranda for their morning nap in the sun.

"Oh, wow, you lot have an easy life," said Tom.

"After we've had a nap we usually go our separate ways until lunchtime. Some of the cats go hunting in the fields up behind the house. A few go across the valley to visit friends, or wander across the field to the house next door to visit the cats that live there. I like to stay near the house and play in the garden and orchard. There are usually lots of things to chase – butterflies, spiders and leaves. We have to be careful and keep our eyes open for snakes and scorpions though. We do have quite a lot of those in Krithoni.

The older cats are very good at catching snakes, but I keep well away from them. Mummy does scream very loudly when she finds a snake that one of the cats has brought home for her. I don't think she likes them very much."

And so the day went by—eating, sleeping, playing, sleeping, eating, sleeping, playing, sleeping—until it was bedtime. Tom thought he could quite easily get used to this life style. He started to walk towards the orchard, thinking he would find a corner somewhere to sleep in, but Mani stopped him, and said, "Where are you going?"

"To find somewhere to sleep, of course," said Tom.

"You are sleeping in the cats' room with us," said Mani. "There is plenty of room, and it is much safer and more comfortable than being outside in the garden."

So, for the very first time in the whole of his life, Tom slept curled up in a warm and comfortable cat bed, indoors, in a house, with a roof over his head.

Next day, after breakfast, Tom and Mani were sunning themselves on the veranda, when Tom gave a long, luxurious stretch, and said, "I have made up my mind, Mani. If you think it will be OK with your Mummy and the rest of the cat family, I would like to stay a while. At my time of life these home comforts are going down very well indeed."

"That is just wonderful, Tom," said Mani. "I know Mummy won't mind. Here she is now."

"Hello Mani. I see your friend Tommy is still here," said Mummy. "Hello Tommy, have you decided to move in with Mani and the others? There is plenty of room for one more cat. Though, we will have to pay a little visit to the v – e – t. Your old wounds need looking at, and you must be neutered if you want to stay here. You do smell a bit unfortunately, like all tomcats, but being neutered will solve that little problem, and you will soon look very handsome, and put a bit of weight on your old bones. Now Mani has settled in again, it is time for me to take him back to the surgery too. While you are both asleep, the doctor will also remove a little piece from the top of your left ears, so that everyone will know that you have been neutered. This time I won't ask any friends to help me. I will carry you both myself on the back of my motorbike."

A few days later Mummy appeared with two cat boxes, one in each hand.

"Oh, no!" said Mani. "Not the cat box again!"

But before he had time to run away, his Mummy had grabbed him and put him in the dreaded box. Then she managed to catch Tom and put him in the other box. She carried them both down to her motorbike, and put the two boxes on the carrier at the back of the bike and securely fastened them so that they could not fall off. She started up the bike and off they went to the animal doctor's surgery.

Mani started to panic, but Tom said, "Hey, don't you worry, I have seen your Mummy taking cats in and out of the surgery, and they come back with a piece of their left ear missing, feeling very sleepy. But the next day they are back to normal again, and after a week or two they all look so well. I am sure she is not going to hurt us, or give us away."

And Tom was right. The vet gave them both an injection to make them sleepy, performed a little operation to neuter them, and then Mummy took Tom and Mani home again to sleep it off. Next day, they were their usual selves and, sure enough, as Tom had predicted, they had both lost the tip of their left ears.

The days drifted by—eating, sleeping, playing, sleeping, eating, sleeping, playing, sleeping—and gradually the hard life that Tom had lived on the wild side began to fade from his memory. The afternoon Siesta time was his favourite part of the day, when Tom would lazily lounge in the shade of the orange trees with Mani and his new family. As he listened to the other cats talking about their lives before their human Mummy had rescued them, he realised that some of them had lived lives even tougher than his had been. What stories they all had to tell.

One evening, a few weeks later, Mani looked at Tom, and said, "Tom, you are looking very handsome! Your wounds have all healed up and your fur has grown again. Your black coat is thick and shiny, and your eyes are bright. You look like a completely new cat!"

"Well, kid, what did I tell you? I saw it happen to some of my old friends in Pandeli. I feel fantastic, like a kitten again. I have so much energy now, and I can almost keep up with you when we are playing

'Chase the Mouse'. I think I will stay here permanently, if that's OK with you. High time I retired from my old hard life on the wild side and took things easy!"

"I am so glad you have decided to stay, Tom," said Mani. "Let's go and tell Mummy and the other cats the good news. Maybe we can have a party tonight to celebrate. I'll ask Sylvester to invite his friends from across the valley."

As the sun disappeared over the hill behind the Leros Cat Hotel, Mani, Tom and all the Krithoni cats gathered together on the veranda for a night of typical cat fun and games. They played tag, climbed trees, and chased anything that moved, until, exhausted from partying, they drifted off to their beds in the Cats' Room and fell asleep to dream of what adventures tomorrow might bring.

The End

Glossary

ANIMAL WELFARE SOCIETIES

In Greece most animal welfare societies are run by foreigners. They rely on donations of money from their supporters and receive no help from the country's government or local councils. They provide shelter and care for animals in need, arrange adoptions of stray cats and dogs, pay for veterinary care, organise vaccination and neutering programmes, and, through education and publicity, encourage responsible animal ownership.

NEUTERING PROGRAMMES

In countries where there are too many cats and dogs that do not have homes, one of the most important contributions to improving the lives of stray and pet animals is to stop them giving birth to unwanted puppies and kittens. For example, a female kitten is ready to give birth at the very young age of five months old, and can give birth to litters of five or more kittens at least three times a year. A female dog can give birth twice a year and can have litters of as many as 10 puppies. A veterinary surgeon performs a simple operation on cats and dogs that stops them from having any more babies. Animal Welfare Societies arrange transport to the vet, look after the animals for several days while they recover from the surgery, and pay the bills.

DODECANESE

The twelve larger Islands in the Dodecanese group are named from the Greek word *dodeka* meaning twelve. There is a total of 162 islands in the group, but only 26 have people living on them.

DRACHMA

The Greek Drachma was replaced by the Euro on 1ˢᵗ January 2002, at a rate of exchange of 340.75 drachmas to €1. At the end of 2001 the rate of exchange to the British pound was 550 drachmas to £1.

FERRY BOATS

Today most of Greece's passenger vessels are ferries which carry cars, lorries, trucks and passengers from ports on the mainland to the islands. Some of the largest ferries carry 2,000 passengers and up to 640 vehicles. Some have very powerful engines and can travel up to 28 knots per hour, which is 32 miles per hour. The ferries from mainland Greece to Leros leave from Piraeus, Athens, and call into the islands of Syros and Patmos, before arriving in Leros. From there they sail on to Kos and Rhodes. They follow the same route in reverse on their way back to Piraeus, Athens. The ferry boats are very important to the islands as they bring everything that the islanders need—food, furniture, electrical goods, building materials etc. There are also smaller boats such as caiques, catamarans and hydrofoils that travel between the islands.

CAIQUES are traditional fishing boats made from wood. Originally they were used for fishing, but today they are used to take tourists on short trips around the islands.

CATAMARAN FERRIES are small high-speed ferries that carry passengers and cars between the islands. Because they have two hulls, they are very stable in rough seas. The catamarans that operate between the islands of the Dodecanese carry up to 337 passengers and 6 vehicles and travel at a maximum speed of 33 knots per hour (38 miles per hour).

HYDROFOILS are small passenger boats that have struts similar to skis. The boat rises up onto the skis, which reduces drag and increases speed. They also operate between the islands during the summer. They travel at 32 knots per hour (37 miles per hour) and carry up to 80 passengers.

GREEK LANGUAGE

Greek, called "el-li-ni-ka" by Greek speakers, is the official language of Greece, and one of the official languages of the Island of Cyprus (the other being Turkish). It is an Indo-European language, with a history spanning 34 centuries. Today it is the native language of about 12 million people, and is spoken worldwide by about 20 million people as their first or second language. The Greek language has made important contributions to humanity in general. The Latin alphabet was based on the Greek alphabet, and more than 150,000 words of the English language are of Greek origin. Most of the International scientific terminologies are Greek. For example:—anthropology from *anthropos* (man), biology from *bios* (life), cardiology from *kardia* (heart).

SOME COMMON GREEK WORDS

Agh-ios/Agh-ia	Saint (pronounced "eye-os"/"eye-a") (male and female)
Ell-a doh	Come here
Evkaris-to (poly)	Thank you (very much)
Ga-ta-ki	Kitten
Ga-to/Ga-ta	Cat (male and female)
Kali-me-ra	Good morning/Good day
Kali-spe-ra	Good afternoon/Good evening
Kali-nik-ta	Goodnight

Kas-tro	Castle
Nay	Yes
Och-i	No (the "ch" is pronounced as in "loch")
Paraka-lo	Please
Tav-er-na	A typical Greek restaurant

KEBABS

Cubes of meat, usually pork or lamb, on a skewer, grilled, and often served with pita bread, which is a flat, round, soft bread.

OLIVE TREES

The fruit of the olive tree, the olive, has been very important to Southern and Southeastern Europe for many years. On the Greek Island of Santorini, fossilised leaves were found that date to about 37,000 years ago. In ancient Greece the wood was used to carve statues and ornaments. The olive leaf was a symbol of abundance, glory and peace, and leafy branches were used to crown the champions in the original Olympic Games. Olive oil was sacred and used to anoint kings and athletes. It was burnt in the sacred lamps of temples and provided the 'eternal flame' of the original Olympic Games. Today it is still used in many religious ceremonies, and research has proved that eating olives and olive oil is very good for our health. Greece is one of several countries well known for exporting olive oil and preserved olives.

ORGANOPHOSPHATE

This is a chemical that kills insects – an insecticide. In some countries, such as Greece, it is used illegally to kill rats and mice because it is cheaper to buy than approved rat poisons. People stuff the insecticide into food and put this down in areas where they know rats feed, such as around chicken runs and rubbish bins. Unfortunately, sometimes dogs or cats will eat the food, often with fatal results.

SCORPIONS

Scorpions are in the same class as spiders – Arachnida – and, like spiders, they have eight legs. The two front legs end with large grasping claws, and they have a narrow segmented tail that ends in a sting. The tail sometimes curves over its back. They are nocturnal, meaning that they come out to hunt at night. During the day they often live in holes in stone walls, so it is not a good idea to put your hand into any holes. There are several species, some are pale yellow/brown in colour, and some are black/brown. Scorpions are found in many countries, especially the warmer countries, such as Greece. The sting of a European Scorpion is not fatal to man, but it is very painful, and if you are unlucky and are stung by one, it is a good idea to visit the nearest doctor or hospital in case you are allergic to the venom.

SNAKES

There are 23 different types of snake in Greece, only six of which are venomous.

Ottoman Viper (Montivipera xanthina)—one of the longest snakes in Greece and found in Thrace and the eastern islands of the Aegean.

Milos Viper (Macrovipera schweitzeri)—only found in some of the western islands of the Cyclades, mainly on Milos.

Horned Viper (Vipera amodytes) – found throughout Greece and the Balkans. Has a small appendix above its nose that looks like a horn.

Adder or Viper (Vipera berus) – Found in northern areas of Greece, bordering FYROM (Former Yugoslav Republic of Macedonia).

Orsini's Viper (Vipera ursinii) – found in some areas of the Pindos Mountains, at altitudes above 1400 meters.

Montpellier Snake (Malpolon insignitus) and **Cat Snake** (Telescopus fallax)—are also venomous but rather harmless because their fangs are at the back of their jaws which makes it very difficult for them to bite man, and the venom is very mild.

CPSIA information can be obtained
at www.ICGtesting.com
Printed in the USA
LVIW020029071012

3077LVUK00007B